5 reasons why we think you'll love this book

To the keeper of this book, an incredible adventure awaits!

Join Maya as she flies through the air to save the day.

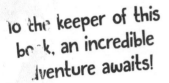

The natural world is full of wonder—turn to the back for fascinating facts!

Meet the beautiful birds of the kingdom and their fairy friends.

Colo...

b...

To the keeper of this book—it's time
for you to visit the magical kingdom
waiting within. Believe in yourself—that
will give you wings to fly!

For Georgia Berry—as brave as Maya and
Willow, and to all her family—Mum, Dad,
Freya and Teddy James.

OXFORD
UNIVERSITY PRESS

Great Clarendon Street, Oxford OX2 6DP
Oxford University Press is a department of the University of Oxford.
It furthers the University's objective of excellence in research, scholarship,
and education by publishing worldwide. Oxford is a registered trade mark of
Oxford University Press in the UK and in certain other countries

Text copyright © Anne Booth 2018
Illustrations copyright © Rosie Butcher 2018
The moral rights of the author have been asserted
Database right Oxford University Press (maker)

First published 2018

British Library Cataloguing in Publication Data

Data available

ISBN: 978-0-19-276621-2

1 3 5 7 9 10 8 6 4 2

Printed in Great Britain
Paper used in the production of this book is a natural,
recyclable product made from wood grown in sustainable forests.
The manufacturing process conforms to the environmental
regulations of the country of origin.

Magical kingdom of Birds

The Sleepy Hummingbirds

ANNE BOOTH

Illustrated by Rosie Butcher

OXFORD

UNIVERSITY PRESS

Chapter One

Maya was sitting in her bedroom, watching a magpie hopping around the garden.

'I heard that when you see a magpie on its own it isn't unlucky for you, it is just unlucky for the magpie because they don't have a friend. So I hope you are lucky and find a friend soon,' Maya said out loud, looking through the glass and out at the handsome black and white bird. Even though he was in the garden, he tilted his head as if he had heard her, and gave a little hop.

'I'm feeling lonely too, Magpie,' said Maya. 'My big sister Lauren is going away to university, and today is her last day at home. I am going to miss her SO much.'

Somehow it helped, saying it out loud. The bird came nearer, looking up at her as if he could understand what she was saying.

'Dad and Penny and Lauren are rushing around, packing up the car and charging up and down the stairs with bags and lamps and things,' Maya went on. 'I'm just getting in the way, and I don't want Lauren to see me feeling sad. She is so excited.'

Maya went over to the pot of peanuts she kept for the garden birds, and then opened the window to get the bird feeder she had stuck on the glass, and topped it up. Instead of being scared by the window opening, the magpie hopped even closer.

'You're beautiful,' said Maya.

Maya loved birds. Her room was full of pictures of them. She had a bird mobile over her bed, binoculars for bird spotting, and lots of books and DVDs about them. Her pencil case had birds on it, her pyjamas and nighties had birds on them, and even the clock on her bedroom wall played a different bird call every hour during the day. Luckily it switched off at night!

One good thing about having a ground-floor room was that Maya could see the garden birds really well. As well as the

bird feeder on the window, there was a bird table right outside. She had already put out fat balls for the birds, because the migrating birds needed to build up energy before their long flight south. Maya knew which birds migrated and which visited or stayed over winter; she knew what special food each type of bird ate, and she spent lots of her pocket money on treats for them.

There was a knock at the door.

'Maya, can I come in?' came Lauren's voice.

'Yes,' said Maya, trying to sound more

cheerful than she felt. She knew that Lauren was so happy to be going away to university, and she wanted to be glad for her, but she couldn't help feeling that nothing was going to be the same any more. Lauren was the best big sister ever.

'Hey, Maya, are you OK?' said Lauren, coming in holding something behind her back.

Maya smiled and nodded, but a big tear escaped and rolled down her cheek.

'Oh Maya—don't cry!' said Lauren. She quickly hid something behind the curtain and went over to Maya to give her a big hug. 'I'll be back before you know it. And I've even got a ground-floor room, like you, so it will be easy for you to visit. It looks onto the university lake, so we'll be able to watch the birds together. I think there might be ducks!'

Maya laughed. Lauren was always showing her funny videos of ducks, and Maya had drawn a duck on Lauren's good luck card. Maya loved drawing birds.

'Now, close your eyes and put out your hands,' said Lauren.

Maya put out her hands and felt

something heavy and flat being put on them. She opened her eyes and saw it was just a simple, brown leather satchel.

'Open it,' said Lauren, smiling.

Maya looked inside the bag and took out what was there. She gasped. It was the most beautiful book she had ever seen. The cover was made from a deep-blue cloth with tiny gold birds all over it, and in gold lettering the title said *Magical Kingdom of Birds*. There were pictures of birds all over the cover, back and front: birds in trees, in forests, in gardens; birds flying over the sea, soaring over mountaintops, diving into rivers; in deserts, in snow; birds in palaces and birds in cottages. Each picture was wonderful in its detail, and the birds were of all different shapes and sizes. Maya had the strangest feeling when she looked at each tiny scene, that it was getting bigger as she gazed at it. It was almost as if she was zooming in on it, like when she looked through her binoculars. She blinked and the pictures went back to normal, but Maya had a funny feeling inside, a feeling that something amazing was going to happen.

She opened the book. The first page
had a detailed picture in black and white,
of a very proud-looking magpie standing
in a woodland clearing.

'It's a colouring book!' said Lauren. 'There are some special colouring pencils to go with it in the bag too. Look, there is something written inside the front cover.'

Maya looked away from the picture of the magpie to the writing.

To the keeper of this book—it's time for you to visit the magical kingdom waiting within. Believe in yourself—that will give you wings to fly!

'It's amazing!' said Maya. 'Where did you get it?'

'From Mum,' said Lauren. 'She gave it to me.'

'Oh Lauren—you can't give it to me, if Mum gave it to you,' said Maya, feeling sad. She wished she could remember her mum the way Lauren could. She had only been little when their mum had died.

'No—you don't understand,' said Lauren. 'Mum gave it to me, with the bag and the pencils, when she was ill and you were a toddler. She said to put it aside safely until you were older, so I put it at the back of my wardrobe. I was just sorting out things for university and felt like now was the right time to give it to you. I hadn't even opened it until today. It's beautiful, isn't it? It's amazing that Mum gave you a bird book when you were a baby, and you know so much about birds!'

'I know!' said Maya. She didn't expect to suddenly feel so happy and excited. Penny was the best stepmother anyone could have, but it was special to know that her mum had been thinking of her, and had got her this book when she was just a baby. How had her mum known she would grow up loving birds so much?

This sad day was turning to something new and wonderful, and Maya knew, deep down, that it was somehow because of this special book.

There was a tap on the window. The magpie was now perched on the back of the garden seat, so that he was really close to the glass.

'Cheeky thing!' laughed Lauren. 'Look, I'll be back later. Sorry we're rushing around so much. I thought you might like to start colouring in a picture while you're waiting. Dad's taking us all out to dinner once the car is packed.'

Lauren left Maya with the book and the bag and the pencils, and Maya hugged the book to her chest.

'Thanks, Mum,' she whispered.

She went to her table by the window. The magpie was still looking in at her.

'Look, there's a big picture of you on the very first page,' she said, holding it up to the window for the magpie to see. 'I wonder what other birds are in it.' She turned the pages. Oddly they were all blank, and, odder still, the book itself kept flicking back to the first page, as if it didn't want her to go any further.

'This is a strange colouring book,' said Maya.

The magpie tapped the glass again. He gazed at her with his shiny black eyes and put his head on one side. Maya had the funniest feeling that both the book and the magpie were telling her to 'get on with it'.

'Well, I won't have to worry about colouring you in wrong!' She laughed. 'You can be my model if you stay still.'

The magpie hopped up and down on the spot, but didn't fly off. He seemed to be watching her.

Maya reached into the bag for the black pen, and started to colour in the book magpie's feathers . . . but as soon as the first feather was finished, something amazing happened. Suddenly, all Maya could see were twirling, tiny, sparkling feathers—first black and white like the magpie's, but then all sorts of browns and reds and oranges and yellows and greens and blues. The glowing feathers swirled around her and somehow she fell into the picture she had been colouring, tumbling and spinning until she found herself sitting, holding the book, on soft green moss in a woodland glade. Next to her was the magpie, now much taller than her. Looking at the flowers and plants around her, Maya could see that it wasn't the magpie who had got bigger, but she who had got smaller.

'It worked! It really worked!' cried a voice, and Maya turned to see a little fairy emerge from underneath a bush. 'The Keeper of the Book has come at last!'

Chapter Two

'**Hello,**' said the little fairy. She had a friendly face, which Maya liked immediately. Her eyes were brown and very kind, and her hair was very curly. She had a big, delighted smile, as if meeting Maya was the most wonderful thing ever, and Maya smiled back—it would have been impossible not to.

The fairy's wings and her long dress were different shades of green. In fact, Maya realized the dress was cleverly woven out of leaves and grass, and she wore a crown of leaves too.

'My name is Willow,' said the fairy. 'I am a fairy princess. And this is Patch, my faithful friend.'

Patch the magpie gave a deep bow.

Maya rubbed her eyes. *Am I dreaming?* she thought. She secretly gave herself a pinch to check. It hurt. This was so odd.

The fairy smiled and nodded encouragingly at her, obviously waiting for Maya to reply.

'My name is Maya,' she said.

'Welcome, Maya, Keeper of the Book,'
said Willow. She put out her hands to
Maya, to help her up.

'Sorry—I don't have my chair or my
stick, and my legs don't work very well, so
it's a bit difficult to get up,' said Maya,
feeling awkward.

'Oh, that's no problem, don't worry,'
said the fairy, and gave her another big
smile, as she sat down next to Maya on
the soft moss. Patch stood in front of
them, almost as if he was on guard.

'You are probably looking at this dress and crown of grass and leaves, and wondering how I can possibly be a princess,' Willow said.

'Well, it isn't what I expected,' said Maya. 'They're beautiful, though.'

'When my father, the king, died,' said Willow, 'my evil uncle, Lord Astor, took over the kingdom. He destroyed my royal cloak of feathers, and he cast a powerful spell on the castle and banished me. Without my cloak of feathers, I am helpless.'

Willow didn't tell her story as if she was

expecting Maya to feel sorry for her, but Maya did.

'That's terrible,' said Maya.

'It is,' said Willow, turning to her, her kind brown eyes serious now, and her face angry. 'Lord Astor hates the way fairies and birds love each other and live in harmony in the kingdom. He wants to imprison all the birds and take them to his castle as slaves. He will keep the ones with the most magical voices or stunning feathers in cages. And I have no power to stop him because he has destroyed my magical cloak of feathers.'

'How awful!' said Maya.

'But you are the Keeper of the Book, Maya, so you can help us!' said Willow, clapping her hands in delight.

'We have an ancient prophecy,' said Patch, the magpie.

Somehow, Maya wasn't surprised that he could talk. It all seemed perfectly normal in this magical land of fairy princesses and enchanted books. After all, he was taller than she was now—or rather, she had shrunk to be smaller than him.

'It says that a girl will come from the human world,' Patch continued. 'She will be the Keeper of the Book, and will fly on a magpie's back and restore the feathered cloak, at a time of great danger for the kingdom.'

'And you must be that girl!' said Willow.

'We have to make the feathered cloak again,' said Patch, 'and we will need your help to collect the feathers.'

'I'll definitely help,' said Maya. 'But I've got a bit of a problem.' She pointed to her legs.

'No problem!' said Willow. 'Hmm, let me see…' She stood, her head to one side, looking at Maya's legs, and then

clapped her hands and laughed. 'Of course—willow! Wait here,' she cried, and she flew off.

'Most of the time you will be flying anyway,' said Patch, matter-of-factly. 'We don't do much walking in the Kingdom of Birds. You will be on my back, as the prophecy said.' He sounded very proud.

Willow flew back and landed, carrying a bundle of things. The first were two beautiful walking sticks. They were light and yet strong, made of woven willow twisted in strands as if they had grown that way, and curved over at the top a bit like a shepherd's crook. Straightaway Maya found them easy to use and she got to her feet.

'And I have made this for you to wear across your shoulder and carry the sticks in,' said Willow, putting a quiver over Maya's shoulder. 'It will carry the sticks the way an archer carries arrows.'

'This is wonderful!' said Maya, putting the bag with the book and pencils in it over her other shoulder.

'I've already woven a harness and a riding seat for Patch, with reins so that you can ride him,' said Willow, and Patch

bent his head so that she could slip it on.

'We knew there would be a lot of flying in this quest, and decided my feathers might be a bit slippery and smooth for the Keeper,' said Patch.

'I hope I can do this,' said Maya. 'I'll do my best. But how will we know how to get the feathers in the first place?'

'I'm sure the book will show us,' said Willow.

Maya was used to riding the ponies in the riding centre near her and got easily on to Patch's back with the help of the light but strong woven sticks. She slotted them into their quiver once she was settled on the riding seat.

'I knew you could!' Patch said. 'The prophecy said you would do it! Now, how is the harness?'

'It feels great!' said Maya, happily, 'I do a lot of riding at home. Though I've never ridden on a bird before! Thank you, Patch and Willow. Let's go and collect the feathers now!'

'It's not that simple,' said Willow. 'You can't beg, borrow, or steal the precious feathers of the magical birds within the kingdom. They must be earned.'

'OK, I will earn them then,' said Maya, her chin lifted up, her eyes bright and determined.

'Oh Maya,' said Willow, giving her a big hug. 'I can't tell you how happy we are that you have come! We have waited so long. We have been calling for the Keeper of the Book for a while now, but our messages didn't seem to get through.'

'I've only just been given the book,' said Maya, feeling awful. 'My sister had it to give me when the time was right, but perhaps she was too busy getting ready for university to realize when that was.'

'It doesn't matter now—you are the perfect Keeper for us,' said Willow, smiling into Maya's eyes. 'I can tell you are brave and resourceful.' Maya felt nervous, but very excited.

'Now,' continued Willow, 'I will tell you what we are going to do. We hear rumours that there is something very strange going on in Hummingbird Garden, so you can consult the book to tell us what it is. Open it and see.'

Maya thought Willow was being a rather bossy princess, but she opened the book anyway, and this time it let her turn

past the page with the magpie. Instead
of it being a blank page, this time it was
a picture of a beautiful tiny hummingbird,
surrounded by huge flowers. But there

was something very odd about the image.

'I've always seen pictures of hummingbirds flying,' said Maya. 'I've never seen a picture of one sleeping on a branch before.'

'This is not good. We must go to the home of the hummingbirds to find out what is wrong,' said Patch.

'Let's go!' said Willow, flying up into the air, her wings an excited blur.

'Everything ready?' said Patch.

'Yes, I'll just make sure everything is safely packed,' said Maya. She put the book back in the satchel. Her hands were trembling. She felt the same as when she had her first ever pony ride, fizzy with excitement.

Patch spread his tail and stretched out his glossy wings on either side of Maya, the white feathers at his wing tips catching the light. He bent forward and leapt up at the same time, Maya tipping slightly on to his feathery neck, and as he did this he beat his wings so that he rose into the air, going higher and higher, up through the trees.

Maya held the reins tightly. She could

feel her own beating heart and the swish of the beautiful bird's feathers as they went. She sat up, sneaking a peep down on to the woodland floor below. Patch expertly weaved his way up, Maya ducking her head at times to avoid a branch, and suddenly, they were clear of the foliage and had burst through into the blue sky above, where Willow was waiting.

Patch hovered, his wings beating steadily.

'Right!' said Willow. 'Are you ready, Maya?'

'Are you still holding on tight?' Patch called back. 'I will be flying as fast as I can.' It was so odd hearing him talk. The ponies at the centre never asked such questions!

'Yes,' said Maya. 'I'm ready.' She had never felt so excited. Lauren had taken her on a ride in a theme park once, and she remembered the funny feeling in her tummy before it began, but this was an even stronger mixture of fear and joy.

'Off we go to the land of the hummingbirds, then!' called Patch. He beat his magnificent wings and, riding on the wind, following the flitting green figure of Willow, they began the most amazing journey Maya had ever been on.

Chapter Three

The ride to the land of the hummingbirds was long, but the seat Willow had made was comfortable, and Maya found it surprisingly easy to get used to riding a huge magpie instead of a pony. She loved the rhythmic swish of Patch's wings and the way he moved through the air, riding the currents. They flew over the tops of many trees, and curious birds flew alongside them—swallows dived and soared, tiny finches flittered, sparrows chirped. Blackbirds whistled alarm calls, and Patch made her laugh as he whistled back an exact imitation, offending a small blackbird, who flew off in a huff.

'You're such a good mimic!' said Maya.

'Why thank you!' he said, but not in his own cheerful voice—this time he was talking in a sneery man's voice that Maya didn't recognize.

'Ugh! Stop it!' said Willow. 'I don't

want to hear your Lord Astor imitation, thank you very much.'

'Sorry!' said Patch in his own voice.

The air was fresh and pure in the Kingdom of Birds, and the further they flew, the warmer it became. Willow mostly flew in front, but often doubled back to check on them or smile at Maya and check she was OK. At one point Maya found her eyes closing and her head nodding, as she leant forward onto Patch's glossy feathers. She opened her eyes with a start, scared she might let go and fall.

'Go ahead and rest,' said Willow, flying up and sitting behind her on Patch's back. Sleepy Maya felt Willow put her arms around her, almost weaving them like branches. Maya stiffened at first and tried to sit up and keep awake. She hated it when people told her to rest, or that she couldn't do something. Maybe Willow was a princess, but she could be just a bit too bossy sometimes.

'You're so brave, Maya. Thank you for coming. I feel that with you beside us, we have a chance to beat Lord Astor,' said Willow. 'We cannot do it without you,

that's for certain. But you must keep your
energy for the task ahead.'

Willow gently took the reins from her,
and, feeling better knowing that Willow
wasn't saying she couldn't do things,
Maya relaxed and let herself sleep.

She woke up, Willow's arms still around
her, to find bright sun on her face. Willow,
once she was sure that Maya was awake,
fluttered ahead, and Patch dived low as
they followed the course of a river by a
forest, their shadows lying on the water
beneath them. Maya noticed what looked

like a beautiful tree full of fluttering rainbow-coloured leaves by the side of the water, but as they passed, the leaves rose up in a noisy cloud of squawking parrots, leaving the branches bare.

'Look!' said Willow, pointing at what seemed to be a swarm of bees or maybe a tornado, twisting up in the air above the trees to their right. Maya could hear what sounded like rushing water or swishing leaves, but as they got nearer she

soon realized from the excited chirps that it was a huge flock of little yellow and green parakeets.

Willow put her hands over her ears and shouted something, but nobody could hear her words over the sound of the birds. She laughed, then shrugged and pointed to the left, and Patch made a swift turn away from the din of the little parrots, and flew back, following the course of the river, into a quiet sky.

At first the quiet was a relief, but as they

flew further away from the parrots the silence felt odd. There were no birds at all flying beside them as they descended. Below them, Maya could see a pair of ornate gates in the middle of a forest, in front of what looked like a beautiful garden full of fruit trees, flowering shrubs, and long tubular red, orange, yellow, and blue flowers.

'You know, hummingbirds do not like unexpected visitors,' said Patch, sounding nervous. 'They may be tiny but they have no fear. I remember a cousin of mine getting a nasty reception when he ran into a crowd of them by mistake.'

'You need have no fear when I am with you,' said Willow, her voice proud. As they approached the garden, Maya could see the excitable fairy had become serious again, aware of her royal duties.

As they flew nearer, the air was full of a sweet perfume and the buzz of insects, but there were no bird sounds. Patch glided down over the gates and landed on the grass.

'Honeysuckle!' called Willow. 'Wake up!'

There, lying on the grass, fast asleep,

was a little golden fairy, dressed in yellow, her wings glowing as the light caught them. Her arms were round a little ruby-red and emerald green bird with a white breast, its feathers shining like tiny jewels in the sunlight. Its head was drawn close to its body, its beak pointing upward, and it looked as if it wasn't breathing.

'Is it dead?' asked Patch.

Honeysuckle opened her eyes. They opened wide and shone blue for a minute.

'Princess Willow!' she said. 'The hummingbirds . . .' and then she fell asleep again.

'What is happening in Hummingbird Garden?' said Willow, in distress. 'Honeysuckle is their fairy guardian—and look at the hummingbirds!' Everywhere around them, on branches or on the ground, were tiny little birds in all sorts of bright colours. Orange, reds and pinks and blues and greens: all motionless, their beaks pointing upwards, their feathers shining in the light.

'They aren't dead—don't worry,' said Maya, pulling her sticks from the quiver and sliding off Patch's back. 'This is torpor—what hummingbirds do when nights are cold. They slow down their breathing so that they can preserve energy, and they look lifeless. But they shouldn't be doing this in the middle of a hot day, they should be flying around licking nectar from the flowers with their little tongues, or catching insects.'

As if to prove her right, there was a scratchy, buzzing, whirring sound and a tiny little bird flew down to one of the flowering shrubs, its wings a blur as it hovered above the flower. Maya knew it was putting its forked, fringed tongue down into the flower to drink the sugary nectar, but it was doing it so fast that an ordinary human eye could never see what was happening. Suddenly it fell, and rolled on the ground under the shrub.

Maya turned one of her sticks around, gently hooked the bird with the top, and drew it out into the open.

Willow knelt beside it and cradled it in her arms.

'Do not drink the nectar, Princess Willow,' it said, weakly. It looked up at Maya and at Patch. 'The prophecy . . . are you the Keeper, come to save us?'

'Yes,' said Maya, 'I think I am. But what has happened?'

'Lord Astor . . . he argued with Honeysuckle, he said he would come and get us all, and bring us to his palace. She said she would never let him. Lord Astor replied that he could do what he liked—that he could even fly here in broad daylight and take us—and we laughed at him and said he would never be able to catch us . . . but he has. I saw the others on the ground, but I knew I had to feed before I could get help. Now I know it was the nectar—he has put a spell on it. I saw Honeysuckle drink it too, before she fell asleep. Please, please help us . . .' Suddenly the little bird went completely still and silent, its beak pointing upwards, like all the others.

'What can we do?' said Willow. 'Lord Astor must be planning to come back to collect them all, and he will bring his guards.'

'How are enchantments broken?' said Maya. 'Can you do magic, Willow?'

'It takes years of skill to learn to undo enchantments. There are magic books in the palace, but Lord Astor has them all now,' said Willow.

'But Maya has the greatest book of all,' said Patch.

Maya took her book out of the satchel and opened it. It fell open at the

hummingbird picture.

'Are there any clues in the drawing?' Maya said. They all looked carefully.

'It's just a picture of what is happening,' said Willow, disappointedly.

'Except . . . except there is no colour in it.' said Maya. 'The book came with coloured pencils. I wonder if I need to use them to find the answer?'

'Well, it's worth a try,' said Patch. 'We have no other option.'

Maya carefully laid the book on a smooth, flat rock in the garden, and, surrounded by sleeping hummingbirds, began to colour in the picture. Maya picked up a red pencil to colour in a particularly tall red flower, and then a blue pencil jumped into her hands and seemed to lead her to a big flowering shrub halfway up the page.

'The pencils seem to want you to colour in particular flowers,' said Willow, 'but I'm not sure why.'

'I don't know either,' said Maya, reaching for an orange pencil, 'but the pencils seem to know something we don't.'

Maya tried to hold the orange pencil, but it rolled away from her. She tried to get a yellow or a blue or a pink, but again, they didn't seem to want her to touch them. The only pencil which would stay in her hand was a silver one.

'There aren't any silver flowers in the garden,' Maya said in exasperation, but the pencil seemed impatient to get on to the page. It led her past the flower which she had intended to colour in, next, to the blue shrub, and up to the top right-hand corner, where you could see the fence at the back of the garden and a bit of the forest beyond. There, in the tiny bit of forest, drawn so small that if the pencil hadn't led her to it she would have missed it, was the outline of a tiny forest creeper with little bell like flowers, and the pencil seemed to hover over them.

As soon as
Maya coloured the flowers
in silver, they flashed and sparkled
and caught the light, and there was
a beautiful, magical chime. Then the
page turned, and instead of
Hummingbird Garden, they were
looking at a picture of the forest
and, in the middle of the page, a
tree with a creeper covered in bell-
like flowers, which were already
coloured in silver and
sparkling and chiming
gently.

'What's happened?' said Patch.

'It's the silver bell flower!' said Willow. 'I remember. My mother told me about it in bedtime stories—it is the one flower in the forest with nectar which can cure enchantments. It only grows in one secret place: on the tallest and oldest tree.'

Maya felt a shiver of excitement. It seemed that the more flowers she coloured in, the braver and more sure of herself she felt.

'Then we must fly and get some silver bell flowers straight away,' said Maya, quickly putting the book and the pencils back in her bag, her sticks back in her quiver, and getting back on Patch's saddle. 'We've got to get that nectar before Lord Astor comes back to get the hummingbirds.'

Chapter Four

'**The** pencils have shown us the direction we should take!' said Maya. 'We must fly through the garden, past the tall red flower and the big blue shrub, down to the back fence. The silver bell flowers are on a tree nearby, in the forest beyond.'

Patch bowed, and then rose up into the air. Maya was used to the sensation this

time, and leant back in her seat, holding the reins and feeling the wind in her hair.

They flew down along through the beautifully coloured and scented garden of the hummingbirds, using the tall red flower and the blue shrub as markers. It was a long and ornate garden, with winding paths, full of flowers and blossoming fruit trees, and even little areas of sand and rock gardens with cacti. Without the markers they could easily have got lost, but thanks to them they found the ornamental back fence, just as it was drawn in the book. Patch soared over it, and Maya looked out for a flash of silver on the trees of the forest. She caught a glimpse of something sparkling, a little way into the trees.

'That way,' she said, pointing so that Patch and Willow could see.

They flew towards the silver sparkles, and as they drew nearer, the sound of tinkling bells became louder and louder.

The trees suddenly thinned out and it became much brighter, as they emerged into a clearing. Willow darted forwards but Maya noticed something in time and, pulling on the reins to warn Patch, quickly got a stick from her quiver and leaned forward, hooking Willow, and pulling her back level with them into the shelter of the trees. Patch fluttered down onto a branch.

'How dare . . .' started Willow indignantly as Maya unhooked her, her face furious and offended, but Maya put her finger to her lips and pointed urgently to the clearing. Willow looked ahead and her expression grew serious as she understood the danger she had nearly run into.

There, in the middle of the clearing, was a huge and ancient tree, tall and

majestic. Its trunk was
covered completely with a
climbing plant which had
thousands of tiny flowers on
it, twinkling and flashing and
chiming softly. But standing in
front of it were two of Lord
Astor's fairy guards.

'Thank you,' whispered Willow. 'You saved me from capture.'

'What can we do?' said Patch.

'Your voice,' said Maya. 'You can distract them and pretend to be Lord Astor! Can you also throw your voice, like a ventriloquist, and make it sound as if it is coming from different places?'

'Yes,' said Patch.

'So, Patch will call out, from the left and then the right, and then when the guards have run off we will swoop in. Patch will fly round the tree, and I will knock off as many silver bells as I can—

and you can catch them in the skirt of your dress, Willow. Does that sound like a good plan?'

'It's the best one we have,' said Willow, nodding.

'Actually, it's the only plan!' said Patch. 'But it's a clever one.'

'Right,' said Maya. 'First, Patch has to convince them that Lord Astor has come. Ready, Patch?'

Patch winked an eye and puffed out his chest.

'YOU, YOU GUARDS THERE. COME HERE IMMEDIATELY!'

Lord Astor's voice rang out, and the guards jumped nervously. The younger one dropped his spear in surprise.

Maya and Willow grinned at each other. Patch was so clever.

'COME HERE I SAY!' shouted Patch as Lord Astor, making his voice come from the left of the tree. The guards set off to the left.

'COME HERE AT ONCE OR THERE WILL BE TROUBLE!' said Patch, making Lord Astor's voice come from the forest on the right this time.

The two guards stopped and shrugged

their shoulders, then the older one pointed to the younger one to run left, and he ran right.

'NOW!' said Maya, and Patch swooped in, Willow flying beside him. Round and round the tree they flew as Maya reached out with her willow sticks and knocked off as many silver bell flowers as she could. Willow flew directly below them and held out her long skirt to catch the falling flowers.

'Hey! You there!' came the voice of the guards. Fairy spears whistled past their ears as they flew away as fast as they could.

Maya had cleared so many vines and branches away with her stick on the way to the clearing that the route to fly back to the garden was obvious. Although they could hear the guards in hot pursuit, flying after them and shouting for part of the way, soon their voices faded.

The garden fence came into view and Patch flew over it, swooping down as Maya and Willow desperately looked for the blue shrub as their first marker.

'There!' Maya pointed, and they headed for the blue foliage and then the tall red flower next to Honeysuckle, the sleeping hummingbird fairy, who was still lying with a motionless hummingbird in her arms.

Before they could get there, however, they saw a tall, thin fairy with grey wings. He was dressed in purple with a golden collar around his neck, and was hovering in the air above the sleeping hummingbirds. The fairy had a huge net in his hands and he was laughing a wicked laugh.

'Ha ha ha ha! So you thought you could beat me . . . Once I've collected all you sleepy birds in my net, I will take you back to my castle. You will look very

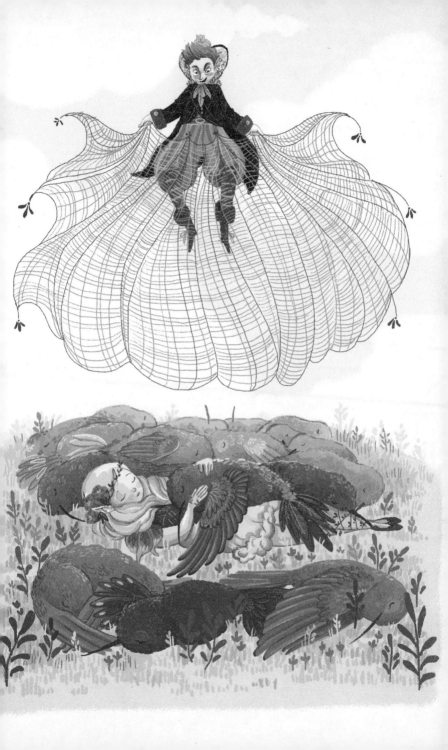

pretty in the new cages I have ready for you and your fairy guardian!'

He dropped the net over the birds with an evil cackle.

Maya took the book out of her satchel and held the bag open.

'Quick!' she said to Willow. 'Empty the flowers into my bag.' Willow poured the silver blossoms from her skirt, chiming as they fell, into the satchel. 'Now, take the book,' said Maya, and handed it to the fairy.

'Patch, swoop down as low and as near the edge of the net as possible,' said

Maya. 'Go—NOW!'

Patch gave a dramatic, fast, and low dive, Maya holding on as tightly as she could, and then, just as he was close to the ground and the net, Maya hurled herself off towards the net, taking Patch and Willow by surprise.

'YOU!' said Lord Astor, turning to see Willow and Patch. He didn't notice Maya, who had now crawled under the net. She gave Honeysuckle the antidote first. The fairy's eyes opened wide but Maya put her finger on her lips before she could speak.

'Don't be scared. I'm with Princess Willow. Lord Astor enchanted the nectar and captured you but we are rescuing you. This is the antidote. He mustn't notice I am here.' Honeysuckle understood immediately, smiled and nodded as Maya crawled from bird to bird and squeezed the precious nectar from the flowers so that it fell in drops into each little bird's throat.

'We must distract him whilst Maya gives the antidote to them all,' whispered Patch to the fairy princess. Willow nodded bravely, and flew up to her evil uncle.

'How dare you treat our birds in this way? You are not fit to be on the throne.'

Lord Astor frowned.

'And how dare YOU talk to me like this, niece! Without your feathered cloak, you are just an ordinary fairy—a nobody. But I am all powerful, and you can't stop me!'

'Just because you sit on the throne, doesn't mean you have a royal heart,' said Willow. 'You do not have the right to rule with cruelty.'

'We will never accept you,' cried Patch, flapping his wings and circling round

Lord Astor. 'Princess Willow is the one we serve!'

'I have cages ready for you in the castle already,' sneered Lord Astor. 'You are no match for me and my army.'

Patch and Willow looked at each other in shock. There was no sign of Maya, and the birds didn't seem to be stirring. Would Maya's plan work? Patch looked at Willow with fear in his eyes.

But then, just as everything seemed lost, they heard an amazing sound.

Chapter Five

'Please wake up!' Maya whispered.

While Willow and Patch were distracting Lord Astor, Maya had been crawling under the net, getting the antidote to each of the birds. At first nothing seemed to be happening . . . and then, one by one, the hummingbirds woke, still a litttle sleepy and groggy.

'What is happening?' they said to each

other, trying to get up.

'Listen to me, all of you,' Maya whispered urgently. Honeysuckle put her finger on her lips and the tiny birds fell silent. 'None of us can walk out of this net,' said Maya. 'But you can all do something together which is far better . . . this is the plan . . .'

'What's that noise?' Willow cried.

There was a low buzzing sound coming from the net below, getting louder and louder—it was the scratchy, whirring, scolding clicks and squeaks of lots of tiny hummingbirds.

'What's happening?' said Lord Astor. 'Noooo!'

At first the net made a funny shape, as if the birds inside were flying in different directions, but then they heard Maya's voice call: 'UP—all of you together—NOW!' The net rose, with a noisy, buzzing, chirping cloud of furious tiny birds inside it.

'Now—fly forwards, until you are over Lord Astor,' called Maya, from her position on the ground. 'Then dive down and out the sides.

Patch and Willow—get out of the way!'

It all happened so fast. One minute Lord Astor was looking up in confusion at the buzzing cloth cloud overhead, the next minute the buzzing intensified, and tiny brightly coloured birds dive-bombed down and out of the sides to freedom, leaving the huge net empty and able to fall neatly over Lord Astor.

'Now, half of you pull the

back ends of the net forward along the ground,' called Maya. Honeysuckle the fairy and Willow flew together, directing the birds to each take a thread at the back of the net, while Patch and the other half of the birds took threads at the front.

'Hey! What are you doing? Ow!' called Lord Astor, as he was bundled up in the huge net and carried high up into the air by hundreds of bright hummingbirds.

Willow flew down and swiftly tied the net with a creeper from a tree. 'All tied up like a parcel!' she laughed.

'Let me out! Let me out!' Lord Astor called, flailing at the bottom of the net, unable to get his balance and stand up straight.

'Not until we get you back to the palace,' said Maya. Willow flew over to Maya and gave her back the book, which Maya placed carefully in her satchel. Patch hopped over and waited while Maya got herself up onto his back again.

'Well done, Maya—that was so brave and clever,' he said. 'You're almost as smart as a magpie!'

'I just knew we could do it,' said Maya, ignoring Patch's boast about magpies. 'Hummingbirds can't walk or even hop really, but they can fly,' said Maya. 'I figured that if I could just crawl under the net and give them each the antidote, then get them to work together, we had a chance.'

Patch bowed, stretched out his wings, and hopped into the air. Maya laughed as they rose higher together and she saw and heard the steady swish and wingbeats of his glossy black and white feathers. Willow flew on ahead with Honeysuckle and the tiny, jewel-bright, noisy birds, carrying the wriggling net, as they crossed the forest and the river, arriving in the air just above a beautiful castle with gardens and a lake.

'This should be my castle,' said Willow crossly, but when Maya looked at her face she looked sad as well as angry.

'All my poor birds . . .' Willow said. 'With Lord Astor in charge they are all in danger.'

She flew next to the net.

'I call on you to surrender, Uncle. Stop this wicked war against my birds, and I will pardon you.'

'Never!' came Lord Astor's furious voice from the net. 'You and that bird and the girl will never get the better of me, Niece. This net can't hold me for ever, and I will be back, you will see. You are too weak to win.'

'Can't we try and get the castle back now?' said Maya. 'Look—we have Lord Astor in a net—we can do anything!'

'No, he is right. Lord Astor and his soldiers are too powerful. I need the enchanted feathered cloak to have the power to rule and defeat them for good,' said Willow, a bit snappily. 'We may have won the battle for the hummingbirds, but we haven't won the war for the kingdom.'

Maya felt a bit hurt. Willow hadn't even thanked her for giving the antidote to the birds. It didn't seem very grateful of Willow to be so cross. Just because she was a princess didn't mean she could be rude. Maya opened her mouth to argue, but Patch spoke at the same time. 'Don't despair, Your Highness,' he said. 'Thanks to Maya, I'm sure we will be able to save the Kingdom of Birds. You will return to the palace one day, I am certain, now we have the Keeper of the Book on our side.'

Willow rubbed her hand across her eyes and flew on ahead, and Maya realized she was crying but was too proud to let them

see. Poor Willow. No wonder she had snapped. It was so hard for her to see the birds in danger and know she still did not have the power to save them all. Maya was glad Patch had interrupted her.

Willow and Honeysuckle and the sparkling birds flew low over the castle lake, nearly to its shore. Suddenly Willow flew in closely and undid the creeper tie around the net, and at her command the birds at one end rose higher than the others, and Lord Astor rolled down the net and fell—with a satisfying *splosh*—into the water.

'Hooray!' said Patch. 'Well done, Your Highness!'

They left him there, soaking wet and wading to the guards at the shore. Lord Astor looked up, red-faced and angry, shaking his fist at them.

'I'll get you, birds! I'll get you, Niece, and that meddling crow and girl. You see if I don't!'

'How dare he!' said Patch. 'I am a magpie, not a common crow. Hold on tight, Maya!' He dive-bombed Lord Astor, so that he staggered back and fell into the water again. The soldiers behind him couldn't help laughing, but when Lord Astor turned around they all looked very serious again.

Patch was very pleased with himself as they soared up to join the others.

'Oh, I am a clever chap,' he said, boastfully.

'Don't crow—or rather, *magpie*,' laughed Maya, but she put her arms around his neck and gave him a hug as she said it. He turned his head so she could see one shiny eye, which he winked at her.

Willow was waiting for them, hovering in the air above, as behind her Honeysuckle and the hummingbirds soared and dived joyfully together in celebration of their freedom.

'That was brilliant, Willow!' giggled Maya. 'Lord Astor definitely deserved that soaking.'

'Thank you, Maya, for everything. You were wonderful. We could never have rescued the hummingbirds without you!'

said Willow, flying up and giving Maya a hug. Her eyes were a little red but her big smile was back on her face. 'I am so sorry I snapped at you. Patch is right. I mustn't despair. You are the Keeper of the Book, and you have answered our call. We have started the fight back.'

'And we will win!' said Patch.

'On behalf of the kingdom, I thank you, Maya, Keeper of the Book,' said Willow regally.

'That's all right,' replied Maya, a little shyly, then Patch suddenly gave a cheeky nosedive, soaring back up in the air and circling round Willow, making them both laugh. Maya looked at Patch and Willow, as they all hovered in the air, and knew she had met two of the best friends she could ever have imagined.

'As princess, I command us all to go back to the Hummingbird Garden and celebrate,' said Willow.

This time Honeysuckle and the hummingbirds flew beside them. The hummingbirds glittered in the sun, their wings a blur, their hum steady, their chirps musical and happy, now that they were free.

When they got back to the garden, the

birds flew straight down to the flowers to drink the unenchanted nectar—the spell had been broken when the antidote had been given. Maya, Willow, and Patch joined Honeysuckle on the soft grass for a picnic. She poured some nectar out into silver goblets for the others to drink, and gave them delicious nectar fairy-cakes to eat.

The hummingbirds gathered around the friends in a happy, humming group.

One of them, an especially tiny one with black and red and greeny-blue feathers, shyly approached them, holding a blue feather in its beak.

'I think little Bee has something to say to you,' said Honeysuckle.

'This is from all of us, to thank you for your help as the Keeper of the Book, and to wish Princess Willow all the luck in the world in her quest to restore the feathered cloak,' said the sweet hummingbird in a tiny but clear voice.

'What a beautiful feather!' said Maya, holding it up and watching how it shimmered and changed colour in the light. 'I've read about hummingbird feathers. They are iridescent. This feather looks different, depending on how the light shines against it.'

'I cannot think of a better first feather for my cloak,' said Willow, beaming.

Maya held it out for Willow to take, but to her surprise Willow shook her head.

'No, Maya. I am afraid that in this world, any feather we earn for the cloak will not be safe. Lord Astor is sure to come back and try to steal it. I must ask you, as the Keeper of the Book, to also be the Keeper of the Feathers. The only

way we can keep it safe is for you to take it home with you.'

'How do I do that?' said Maya, feeling sad to leave this magical world and her new friends so soon.

'Place the feather in the book and it will take you back to your world,' said Willow.

'But you will come back to help us find the next feather,' said Patch quickly, noting the expression on Maya's face. 'You alone are the Keeper of the Book and I alone am the magpie you ride on, as the prophecy said.' He puffed out his chest as he said it, and the hummingbirds hummed admiringly around him.

Willow and Honeysuckle flung their arms around Maya in a warm hug.

Patch bent his head so she could reach up and stroke it. He put his head on one side in a cheeky way, and his eyes sparkled.

'Until the next time, Maya,' he said.

Maya took a deep breath and opened the book. It turned to a blank page and she placed the feather on it. The page began to glow and then, just as at the beginning, iridescent, shimmering feathers and black and white magpie ones whirled round and round until Maya found herself back in her chair, sitting at her table, the open book in front of her. But the page was not blank any longer—it was full of a colourful scene of hummingbirds whizzing round a garden, just as they should be, their long bills deep down in beautiful flowers, and lying on the page was a tiny glowing feather.

'Look how tiny it is in real life!' said Maya. 'How am I going to be able to keep it safe?' As she spoke, the feather on the page seemed to change, and turned into a drawing itself.

'Thank you, magic book,' laughed Maya. 'You are so clever.'

'Maya!' Lauren was knocking at the door. 'We're all packed now. Dad wants to take us out for dinner. Can I come in?'

'Yes, yes of course,' said Maya. It felt so strange to be back to normal life.

Lauren's eyes glanced down at the brightly coloured scene in the book. She smiled and hugged Maya.

'You've done a great job with that colouring in, Maya.'

Maya looked down at the page. The birds almost seemed to flutter and move in the light.

'Lauren, what did Mum say to you when she handed you the book?'

'She said she loved us both very much,

and she was sure that we were each going to have adventures only we could have. And that is true, Maya,' said Lauren, giving her little sister a big hug. 'I am going off to have my adventures at university, and I know I will miss you very much, but I also know you are very special, Maya, and you are going to have adventures yourself that only you—not I—can have.'

'Come on girls!' called Penny from the hallway.

'Are you ready to go?' called Dad.

'Yes!' said Lauren and Maya together.

They looked at each other and laughed.

And Maya, looking over at the book and the pencils on the desk, thought of all the other feathers she and Patch and Willow had to collect, and the exciting adventures they would have together.

'I just can't wait to see what happens next!' she said.

Acknowledgements

I would like to thank OUP for giving me the opportunity to write this series—I am having such fun finding out about all the birds Maya meets. For this book I have been using websites such as the RSPB's, and watching videos of hummingbirds on YouTube and reading as much as I can about them. I have looked up websites about the plants people grow to attract hummingbirds, and hope one day to travel to a country and see them in the wild.

I would like to thank my friend Helen Sole, teacher, play therapist and someone who played for Great Britain Sitting Volleyball Team, for editorial advice on Maya's problems with her legs.

Thank you to Liz Cross, Clare Whitston, Gillian Sore and Debbie Sims at OUP for all their work on this series, and to all at OUP behind the scenes who support the books in any way.

Thank you to the wonderful illustrator Rosie Butcher who brought the Magical Kingdom to life, and to the talented designer Lizzie Smart for making the books look so beautiful.

Thank you to my husband Graeme and my children Joanna, Michael, Laura and Christina for all their love and support and for patiently listening to me reading out bits of my books, sharing exciting things I find out about birds and asking advice about changes in storylines!

And to my dogs Ben and Timmy, who are excellent company for a writer.

About Anne

Every Christmas, Anne used to ask for a dog. She had to wait many years, but now she has two dogs, called Timmy and Ben. Timmy is a big, gentle golden retriever who loves people and food and is scared of cats. Ben is a small brown and white cavalier King Charles spaniel who is a bit like a cat because he curls up in the warmest places and bosses Timmy about. He snuffles and snorts quite a lot and you can tell what he is feeling by the way he walks. He has a particularly pleased patter when he has stolen something he shouldn't have, which gives him away immediately. Anne lives in a village in Kent and is not afraid of spiders.

About Rosie

Rosie lives in a little town in East Yorkshire with her husband and daughter. She draws and paints by night, but by day she builds dens on the sofa, watches films about princesses and attends tea parties. Rosie enjoys walking and having long conversations with her little girl, Penelope. They usually discuss important things like spider webs, birds, and prickly leaves.

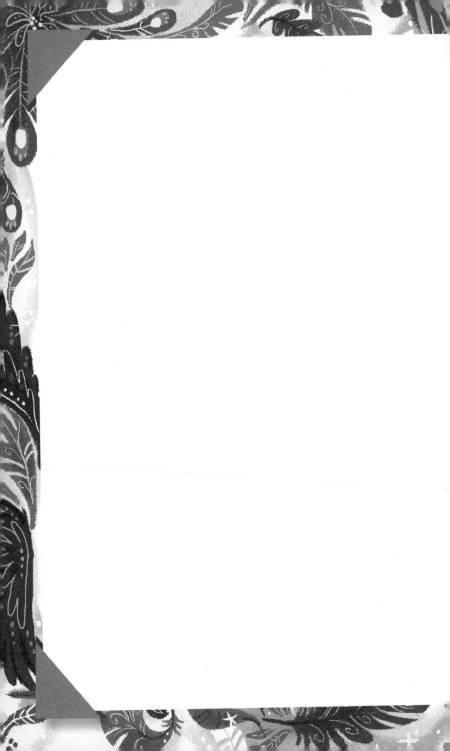

Bird Fact File

Turn the page for information
on the real-life birds that
inspired this story.

Fun Facts

Find out all about these tiny,
colourful, and cute birds!

1. Bee hummingbirds are the smallest birds
in the world! They can be as tiny as 57mm
in length.

2. Male bee hummingbirds weigh about 1.6g.
That's lighter than a 1p coin!

3. Hummingbirds are really fast birds. When they dive to catch food, they move as fast as 60mph!

4. Hummingbird wings can flap up to 200 times in a second when they're flying, so if you watch a hummingbird, its wings are all a blur.

5. A hummingbird's heart beats at around 1200 times each minute. That's about 15 times faster than a human's.

6. Hummingbirds have almost no sense of smell. Instead, they use their very good eyesight to spot food and other hummingbirds.

7. Some hummingbirds eat half their own weight in food every day. They can even drink 8 times their weight in water.

8. Hummingbirds are amazing flyers. They can hover, fly backwards, and even fly upside down!

9. They have feet so tiny that they cannot walk on the ground, and find it awkward to shuffle along a perch.

10. Just like in the story, a hummingbird's main food source is nectar, although they may catch an insect now and then for a protein boost.

11. Hummingbirds can hover at the opening of flowers and extend their long tongue to reach the nectar inside.

12. A hummingbird's tongue is grooved like the shape of a "W", to help lap up nectar from flowers.

13. Hummingbirds fly by beating their wings in a figure-of-eight. These speedy wing movements produce the humming noise that this species is known for.

14. Although hummingbirds are teeny, they are very territorial and have been known to chase off other birds as big as hawks from their home.

15. The vervain hummingbird lays the world's smallest bird egg, just 1cm long and weighing 0.3g.

16. A hummingbird's brain is 4.2% of its body weight, the largest proportion in the bird kingdom.

Where do you find hummingbirds?

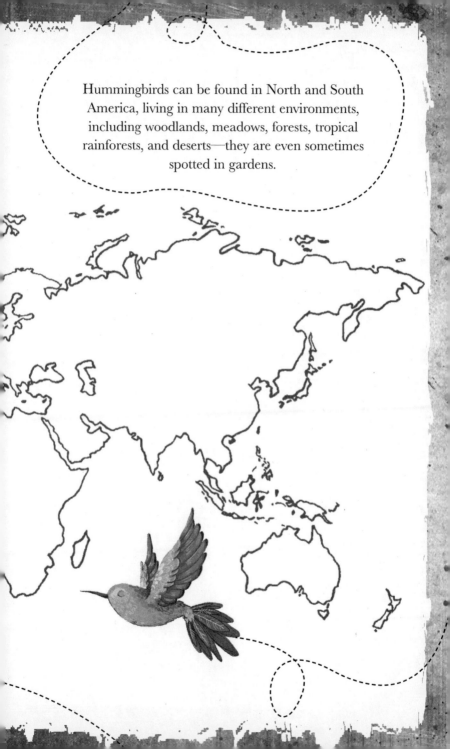

Hummingbirds can be found in North and South America, living in many different environments, including woodlands, meadows, forests, tropical rainforests, and deserts—they are even sometimes spotted in gardens.

Turn the page for some fantastic

Bird activities

Make a brilliant bird snack skewer!

Follow these steps to make a super snack for
the birds in your garden.

Make sure an adult is helping you with this,
as some steps are a bit fiddly.

YOU WILL NEED:

- Floral wire (available from most garden centres and craft shops)

- Bird food (e.g. apple, stale bread, hard cheese, raisins)— check the RSPCA website for other great bird-friendly foods

- String

Make your skewer

Step 1

Get the ingredients you want to put on your skewer. Apples, stale bread, hard cheese, and raisins are all great ideas.

Step 2

Cut your ingredients into small cube-sized pieces. Make sure an adult is doing the cutting and don't use a knife yourself.

Step 3

Push the fruit, bread, and cheese onto pieces of floral wire, leaving about 10cm of uncovered wire at either end.

Step 4

Bend the ends of the wire into hooks.

Step 5

Now bend the wire into a circle, linking the hooked ends together.

Step 6

Tie a loop of string around your wire skewer circle and hang it outside.

Step 7

Watch your garden's birds enjoy their lovely skewer snack!

Make a tasty bird-shaped biscuit!

These tasty treats are great for
a lunchbox snack.

Ovens get very hot and sharp equipment
is needed for this, so make sure you have
an adult helping you.

You will need:

Biscuit ingredients
- 100g butter, softened
- 100g caster sugar
- 1 medium-sized egg, lightly beaten
- 275g plain flour
- 1 tsp vanilla extract

Icing ingredients
- 400g icing sugar
- 3-4 tbsp water
- 2-3 drops food colouring

Step 1

Heat your oven to 190°C/ Gas 5 and line a tray with baking paper

Step 2

Cream the butter and sugar together.

Step 3

Slowly beat in the vanilla extract and egg until the mixture is well-combined.

Step 4

Stir in the flour until a
dough is formed.

Step 5

Roll the dough out to
1cm thickness on a
lightly floured clean
surface.

Step 6

Using a bird biscuit cutter or
a small knife, cut small bird
shapes out of the dough and
gently place these onto the
baking tray.

Step 7

Bake the biscuits in the oven for 8-10 minutes. They should be a light gold colour. Next, take the biscuits out of the oven and leave to cool for 5 minutes, and then place them on a wire cooling rack.

Step 8

To make the icing, sift the icing sugar into a bowl and add water, stirring it in, until a smooth mixture is created. Then stir in the food colouring.

Step 9

You could make all sorts of birds at this stage! Pick your favourite species or make up a new magical kind of bird.

Step 10

Spread the icing gently onto the biscuits using a knife or a large spoon and leave until the icing has hardened.

Join Maya for a new adventure in

The Ice Swans

The Magical Kingdom of Birds is in
trouble! Wicked Lord Astor has frozen Swan
Lake and turned its beautiful swans
into statues. Can Maya, with the help of her
friends Willow and Patch, break the
enchantment and save the day?

Chapter One

'Maya—don't forget to get ready for skating!' Penny called from the kitchen. 'You'll need a warm coat and hat and gloves for the outside rink.' It was Saturday afternoon, when normally Maya and her big sister Lauren would do things together, but Lauren had gone away to university, and Maya's dad and stepmum Penny were taking her out for a special treat. The trouble was, Maya didn't want to go.

'I'll never be able to ice skate,' said Maya to her dad, knowing Penny couldn't hear. 'I know Penny loved it when she was my age, but she should know that her legs worked better than mine. I know I'll just look silly. I'll hate it and I won't be any good, so what's the point?'

'Don't say that, love,' said her dad. 'Look at how good you have got at riding.'

But Maya wasn't listening to her dad.

'Why did Penny sign me up for those stupid lessons anyway?' she grumbled, putting on her hat.

'She's worried you are missing your big sister now she has moved out. She thought ice skating would be something fun you could do together,' said Dad.

'Are you ready, Maya?' said Penny, coming into the hall. 'Where are your gloves?'

'In my room I think. I'll go and get them,' said Maya.

'Be quick!' called Penny. 'My friend can't wait to meet you. She is such a great teacher, she'll have you whizzing round the ice rink in no time at all. It's going to be such fun.'

'For you, maybe, not for me,' Maya said under her breath, as she went into her room.

She didn't mean to slam the door quite so hard behind her, but it crashed shut and the satchel on the back of the door fell off. Some pencils and a large book fell out and rolled across the floor.

'Oh no,' said Maya. She managed to pick up the colouring pencils and put them back into the satchel. Then she

picked up the book and carried it over to the table by the window to check it hadn't been damaged.

'I'm so sorry,' she said to the book. It was an extraordinarily beautiful book, covered in deep blue cloth with tiny shimmering golden pictures of all sorts of birds. The book itself seemed to glow and tingle in her hands as she spoke to it, and Maya felt her heart beat a little faster. Maybe it was time. Maybe the book hadn't fallen off because she had slammed the door. Maybe it had fallen off because today, at last, she would be allowed back into the Kingdom of Birds. She had already had one adventure in the Kingdom and she knew there were more waiting for her, but she couldn't go back unless the book showed her a magic picture to colour in.

'I'd much rather be riding Patch the Magpie than looking silly falling over on the ice,' said Maya, as she picked up her red woolen gloves and pulled them on. 'I'm the Keeper of the Book after all, and I need to get back to help Princess Willow regain her kingdom.' She put the book on the table and glanced out of the

window. Suddenly she saw a big black and white bird fly into the garden. It was a magpie, and it swooped low over the grass and landed just near the window. It tilted its head, its black eyes shining, and seemed to Maya to give her a nod.

'My friends must be ready for me,' she thought and, taking a deep breath, she opened the book. 'Please, magic book, let there be a picture this time.'

She had looked in the book every day since she last visited the kingdom, but the pages had been blank. This time though she was not disappointed. The book fell open on a picture of an icy tower on a frozen lake. The tower was surrounded by ice sculptures of swans, some big, some very little.

Maya grabbed an ice blue pencil and began to shade in the tower. She could feel that something incredible was about to happen. Suddenly, all she could see in front of her were whirling, glittering, sparkling, white and black feathers and a cloud of glittering snow. This was how she had entered the Kingdom of Birds the first time, so she wasn't scared when she was lifted up into the air, and found herself falling into the picture she had been colouring, tumbling and spinning down into the sparkling magic.

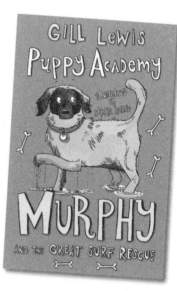